4 Easy-to-Read Stories

Care Bears™: *How Does Your Garden Grow?*
Care Bears™: *Journey to Joke-a-Lot*
Care Bears™: *Most Valuable Bear*
Care Bears™: *Winter Wonderland*

SCHOLASTIC INC.

New York   Toronto   London   Auckland   Sydney
Mexico City   New Delhi   Hong Kong   Buenos Aires

Care Bears™: *How Does Your Garden Grow?* (0-439-54962-0)
CARE BEARS™ © 2003 Those Characters From Cleveland, Inc.

Care Bears™: *Journey to Joke-a-Lot* (0-439-65102-6)
CARE BEARS™ © 2004 Those Characters From Cleveland, Inc.

Care Bears™: *Most Valuable Bear* (0-439-66958-8)
CARE BEARS™ © 2004 Those Characters From Cleveland, Inc.

Care Bears™: *Winter Wonderland* (0-439-66959-6)
CARE BEARS™ © 2005 Those Characters From Cleveland, Inc.

ISBN 0-439-76310-X

12 11 10 9 8 7 6 5 4 3 2 1   5 6 7 8 9 10/0
Printed in the U.S.A. 56 • This compilation edition first printing, June 2005

Care Bears™

How Does Your Garden Grow?

by **Frances Ann Ladd**

Illustrated by **Jay Johnson**

"It is a beautiful day,"
said Funshine Bear.
"What should we do?"

"Let's plant a garden,"
said Cheer Bear.

"Let's make it a
rainbow-colored garden!"
said Bedtime Bear.

"Good idea!"
said Friend Bear.

The Care Bears went
to find their seeds.

"I like pink tulips,"
said Cheer Bear.
"The bulbs are
in my pot."

"I will grow
yellow sunflowers,"
said Funshine Bear.
"The seeds are
in my bucket."

"Can I plant green
four-leaf clovers?"
asked Good Luck Bear.

"Of course!"
said Friend Bear.

"Oh, no!" said Friend Bear.

"My bucket of daisy seeds is gone."

"Here it is," said Good Luck Bear.

"No," said Friend Bear.
"That's Bedtime Bear's
bucket of sweet dreams."

The Care Bears met
at the Cloud Patch.
"What is wrong?"
asked Wish Bear.

"I can't find
my daisy seeds,"
said Friend Bear.

"I wish you could find them,"
said Wish Bear.

"That's okay," said Friend Bear.
"I can help you plant your seeds."

"Let me help you
dig your holes,"
said Friend Bear.

"Thank you,"
said Love-a-lot Bear.

"You look sleepy,"
said Friend Bear.
"I can plant your seeds."

"That is a big help,"
yawned Bedtime Bear.

"May I water that row?"
asked Friend Bear.

"Yes, please,"
said Good Luck Bear.

Soon, the Care Bears were done.
"Thank you for your help,"
Funshine Bear said to Friend Bear.

"We couldn't have done it
without you," said Cheer Bear.
And the Care Bears went to play.

That night, Bedtime Bear
sprinkled sweet dreams
on the garden.

Then he looked at his bucket.
"Uh-oh," said Bedtime Bear.
"This is not my bucket."

Many weeks passed.
The garden grew.
Friend Bear got a big surprise.

"How did my daisies grow?"
asked Friend Bear.
"I wish I knew," said Wish Bear.

"I know," said Friend Bear.
"It was Bedtime Bear.
Our buckets got mixed up."

"He sprinkled daisies
instead of dreams."

"Maybe," said Love-a-lot Bear. "Or maybe your friendship helps everything grow!"

Journey to Joke-a-lot

by **Frances Ann Ladd**
Illustrated by **Jay Johnson**

Grumpy Bear built
a Rainbow Carousel.

But the carousel
spun too fast.
"Make it stop!"
cried the Care Bears.

The carousel fell to pieces.
Grumpy Bear needed cheering up.

Funshine Bear made jokes.
Grumpy Bear felt worse.

"'Cheering up' is not 'making fun of,'"
Grumpy Bear said.
"If you do not know that,
you do not belong here."

"Maybe I should leave,"
said Funshine Bear.

Then he ran away.

Funshine Bear found
a car in the woods.
The car took him
on a wild ride.

The car landed
with a THUD!

"Where am I?"
asked Funshine Bear.
"You are in Joke-a-lot,"
said a pig named Gig.

"Look!" Funnybone shouted.
"He has the royal birthmark.
He is the long-lost
King of Joke-a-lot."

"Long live King Funshine Bear!"
cried all of Joke-a-lot.

Funshine Bear loved Joke-a-lot.
He could laugh and joke
all day long.

The Care Bears came
to get Funshine Bear.
"It is time to come home,"
said Tenderheart Bear.

Funshine Bear did not know
if he wanted to go home.
"I like being king," he said.

Funshine Bear slipped
on a banana peel.

He fell into a giant cake.
Everybody laughed.

"That was funny,"
Funshine Bear said.
"But please help me
out of this cake."

"It is good to have fun,"
said Funshine Bear.

"But you also need to
listen to others and
think about their feelings."

Funshine Bear wanted to go home.
"As long as I have my friends,"
Funshine Bear said,
"I will always be a king."

Most Valuable Bear

by **Justin Spelvin**

Illustrated by **Jay Johnson**

Champ Bear woke up
bright and early.

It was the perfect day
to do something special.

"Let's play baseball!"
he said to his friends.

"That's a great idea!"
said Good Luck Bear.

"But what if I can't play?"
worried Grumpy Bear.

"I know," said Champ Bear.
"I can teach you!"

"First, you pitch the ball,"
said Champ Bear.

He threw fast and straight.
"Wow!" said Good Luck Bear.

"Next, you hit the ball,"
added Champ Bear.

He swung his bat and hit.
The ball flew far and away.
"Can I try?" asked Cheer Bear.

But Champ Bear was not done.
"Then you have to run
around the bases," he said.

"I could do that," said Grumpy Bear.

"You also have to catch,"
said Champ Bear.
He threw a ball in the air
and then caught it.

"We're ready to play,"
Good Luck Bear said.
"I want to swing the bat,"
Cheer Bear said.

"I bet I could catch,"
Wish Bear said.

But Champ Bear didn't hear
any of his friends.

Champ Bear was still pitching,
hitting, running, and catching.

So his friends just sat
and watched.

"Playing baseball is not much fun," said Grumpy Bear.

Champ Bear finally stopped.
"I sure am tired," he said.
"Why do you look so sad?"

"You're a great teacher,"
said Cheer Bear.
"But you were so busy
showing us how to play…"

"That none of us got to try,"
Grumpy Bear added.

Share Bear knew what to do.
"If we played as a team,
we could share the fun!"

"And you wouldn't be so tired,"
added Good Luck Bear.

And that's just what they did.
For the rest of the day
they threw, hit, ran,
and caught as a team.

"Thanks for a great game!"
cheered the Care Bears.

CareBears™

Winter Wonderland

by **Justin Spelvin**

Illustrated by **Jay Johnson**

A snowflake landed
on Tenderheart Bear.

"The first snow!"
he cheered. "It's time for
the Winter Festival!"

There was so much to do.
Tenderheart Bear made a list.

He gave each bear a job.

"What can I do?"
Cheer Bear asked.

"Come with me,"
Tenderheart Bear said.
"I'll find you a job."

Share Bear's job was snacks.
"I wanted to make snow cakes,"
said Share Bear.
"But I only have chocolate icing!"

SUGAR

"I know," said Cheer Bear.
"Sprinkle sugar on top."

"Great idea!" said Share Bear.

Wish Bear's job was music.
"I can't find my radio,"
said Wish Bear.

"What will we do?" asked
Tenderheart Bear.

"We could all sing,"
said Cheer Bear.

"Yes," said Wish Bear.
"And I have just the right song."

Champ Care Bear's job
was cleaning the ice.

"We can't go ice-skating,"
Champ said sadly.
"The pond's not frozen yet."

"I know," Cheer Bear said.
"We can roller-skate instead."

"What a good idea!"
said Champ Bear.

Grumpy Bear's job
was building snowbears.

"Oh, dear," said Grumpy Bear.
"This is too heavy for me."

"We can all try,"
Cheer Bear said.
"One, two, three . . ."

The head fit just right.
"Thanks," said Grumpy Bear.

The big festival banner
hung from the trees.

CARE-A-LOT
FESTI

"What else should I put up?"
Bedtime Bear asked.

WINTER
VAL

SWEET
DREAMS

"Stars are cheery,"
said Cheer Bear.
It was a great idea.

So they hung stars
from every tree.

"I never got a job,"
said Cheer Bear.

"No, not one job,"
Tenderheart Bear said.
"Instead, you helped us all!"

Cheer Bear smiled.

Soon Care-a-lot was filled
with singing, roller-skating,
snowbears, and tasty treats.

CARE-A-LOT WINTER
FESTIVAL

It was the best
Winter Festival ever.

CARE-A-LOT WINTER
FESTIVAL